94 0317

DATE DUE

GAYLORD   PRINTED IN U.S.A.

XYZ *Adventure*

in Alphabet Town

by Janet McDonnell
illustrated by Linda Hohag

created by Wing Park Publishers

 CHILDRENS PRESS ®

CHICAGO

Library of Congress Cataloging-in-Publication Data

McDonnell, Janet, 1962-
    An XYZ adventure in Alphabet Town / by Janet McDonnell ;
illustrated by Linda Hohag.
       p.   cm. — (Read around Alphabet Town)
    Summary: Three friends, Xavier, Yoko, and Zelda, fight about
which letter is best, but finally come to agree that they all are the
best.
    ISBN 0-516-05424-4
    [1. Friendship—Fiction.   2. Alphabet.] I. Hohag, Linda, ill. II.
Title.   III. Series.
PZ7.M1547Xy   1992
[E]—dc 20
                                      92-2985
                                         CIP
                                          AC

XYZ *Adventure*
in Alphabet Town

You are now entering Alphabet Town.
With houses from "A" to "Z."
There's an "XYZ" adventure today.
Come, see what fun it will be.

These are the "XYZ" houses of
Alphabet Town. Xavier, Yoko, and
Zelda live here.

They live side by side. They are
friends. But sometimes they do not
get along.

They fight about which letter is best.

Xavier thinks "x" is best. He likes
anything that has the sound of "x."

He likes to look for "EXIT" signs.

And he likes to exercise.

Once he ate six boxes of cookies.
Then he did extra exercises.

" 'X' is excellent!" Xavier always says.
"You can use 'x' to mark the spot.

"And 'X' is for

X-ray.

X-rays let you see your bones.

"The letter 'x' is the best," says Xavier. "I know because I am an expert."

"You are wrong," Yoko says.
"My letter 'y' is the best of all.

"Without 'y' you can not tell
yummy food from yucky food.

"But with a 'y' you can play in your yard with a

yo-yo.

Or you can paint your house

yellow.

''You can yodel with a

yak.

And best of all, you can yell

yahoo!

Yes, 'y' is the best letter of all.''

"No, no, no," Zelda says. "My letter is better.

''With a 'z' you can zip up your

zipper.

"And you can go to the zoo. What would you do without the zoo?

"Without a 'z,' a zebra would just
be a horse.

"But with a 'z,' you can zig-zag,
and zoom,

and zip all around. 'Z' is the
best letter of all.''

"I have an idea," says Xavier one day. "Maybe 'x,' 'y,' and 'z' are all the best."

"Yes, I agree," says Zelda. "Perhaps
we really need all three."
"Yahoo!" yells Yoko. "And maybe
now we can live happily ever after."

MORE FUN WITH
XAVIER, YOKO, and ZELDA

What's in a Name?

In our adventure, you read many "x," "y," and "z" words. Our names begin with these letters. Not many names begin with them, but here are a few.

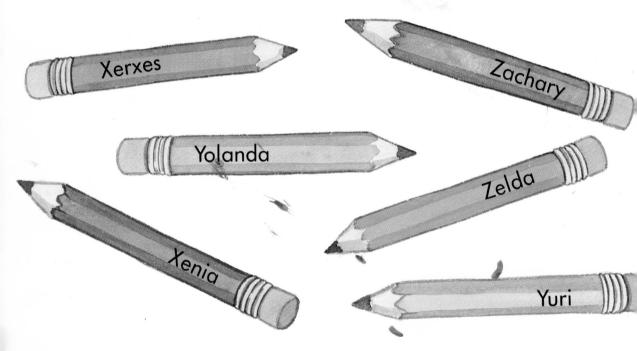

Xerxes

Zachary

Yolanda

Zelda

Xenia

Yuri

Do you know other names that begin with these letters?

Does your name start with one of them?

X, Y, Z Word Hunt

We like to hunt for words with "x," "y," or "z" in them. Can you help us find a word on this page that begins with "x"? With "y"? With "z"?

buzz

fox

candy

taxi

razor

yarn

zero

xylophone

royal

Can you find a word with "x" in the middle?
How about one with "y" in the middle? One with "z"?
Now can you help us find a word that ends with "x"?
With "y"? With "z"?